ReadZone Books Limited

50 Godfrey Avenue
Twickenham
TW2 7PF
UK

Visit our website: www.readzonebooks.com

Fred
and
Finn

by Madeline Goodey

illustrated by Mike Gordon

Fat frog Finn and
thin frog Fred
were jumping up
and down.

Along came a fly.

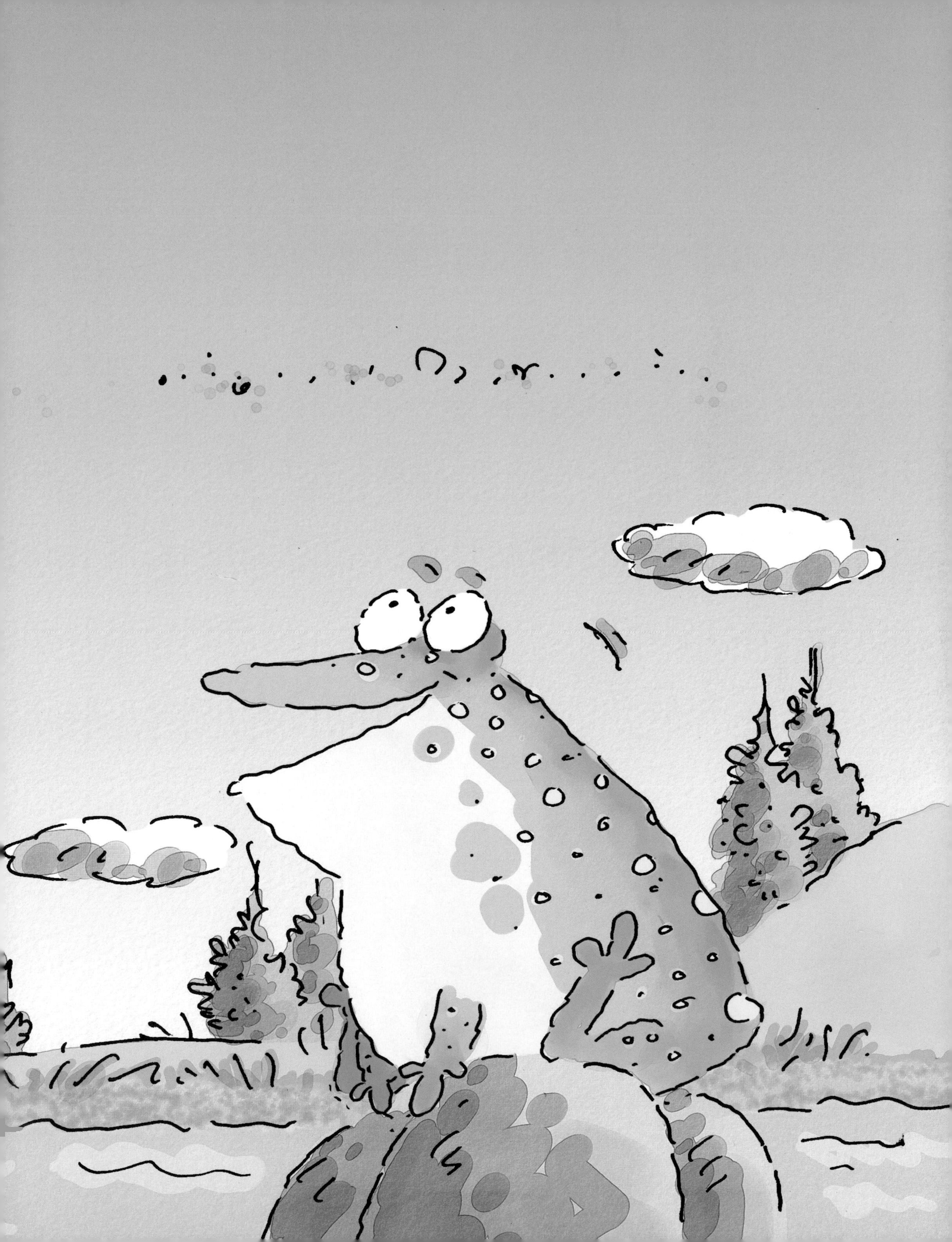

Up jumped fat Finn and
grabbed that tasty fly!

Thin Fred was too slow.

Along came a slippery slug.

Down jumped fat Finn and ...

... gobbled up that slippery slug.

Thin frog Fred was too slow,
again.

Along came a
lovely bug.

Under the branch
jumped fat frog Finn ...

... and got stuck!
He couldn't move.

Thin frog Fred jumped over
the branch and ate that
lovely bug. At last!

Fat frog Finn could not move.

Thin frog Fred munched
on a juicy caterpillar.

Fat frog Finn still could
not move.

Thin frog Fred had a berry for his pudding.

So fat frog Finn got thin and
thin frog Fred got fat!

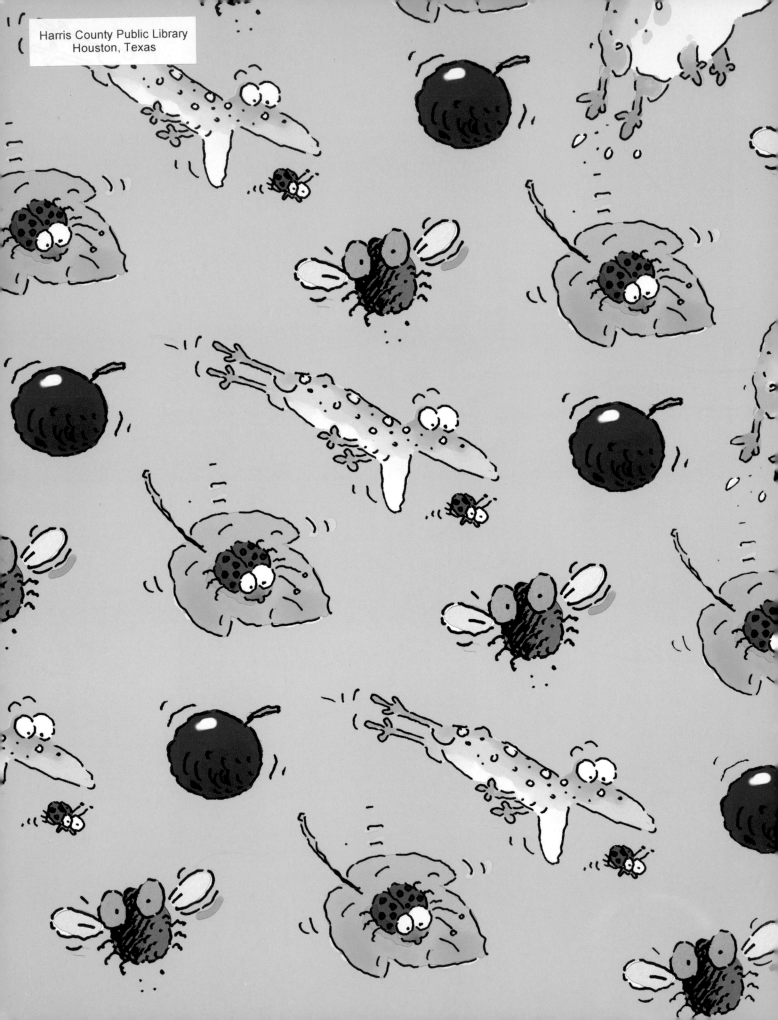